# The Gift Garden

Kenny Mooney

__FLAT__FIELD__PRESS__

For Francesca

# The Gift Garden

*But I am a blasted tree; the bolt has entered my soul; and I felt then that I should survive to exhibit what I shall soon cease to be - a miserable spectacle of wrecked humanity, pitiable to others and intolerable to myself.*

Mary Shelley, *Frankenstein*

ALL
DISEASE
AND
MOLD

My doubt is a festering wound. It leaks infection into my body, spreading through the good parts of me that I know remain. It is always there, somewhere. It is a parasite, a corrupt outgrowth of me. It lives in the darkest parts, the hidden parts, always looking for signs, for evidence. I stutter insults under its control, throwing out rage and bitterness into all the rooms of the apartment. That poison sinks deep into the furniture, slowly disintegrating everything. The wallpaper yellows and strips back revealing bare plaster walls, stained by the thick black ink I spew. Holes appear in the armchairs, in the carpet. They grow and spread as I infect the air. I sit in the bedroom and chew on the nylon, weeping tears of black.

These days my thoughts rage like a fire. Moods

change like neon signs flickering. I toss and turn. Thrash and moan. A poison surges in these veins; it makes me sick. I grow dark and weary with me. I tire of my own thoughts.

I dwell on her in these nights of burning. Dwell on what I know, what I don't know. I pick apart her history, those others, the lovers who came before. Those I don't know about now. It tears me apart, those images I can't control. They play through in slow motion, rewind, repeat.

These days she seems more like a visitor to my life, less like my lover. She comes to me during these nights, she sleeps in our bed, but the days I am left alone. She leaves me for her work in the hospital, and returns each day with strange smells. Her body forms shapes with suspicious angles. I pace the apartment floors all day, those thoughts plaguing me, questions and more questions. I am incapable of living beyond this.

And so my moods reel, from desperation to anxiety to fury. I get lost in my own paranoia, in a maze of emotions I am ill-equipped to deal with. If I could talk to her she would listen, I know, but the words won't form in my mouth. My lips move silently. Make shapes in the night while I watch her sleep, but no sound emerges. I stuff her clothing into my mouth to soak up this shit. This shit of failure.

So I rage and ramble at myself. Cry and berate myself. I blame her and I blame me. She is completely unaware of any of it. She never seems to even notice the pain I feel. Whether she ignores all those terrible words I throw, or she is incapable of hearing them, I don't know. Gliding softly through it all, the fog of my war invisible to her, she glows a pristine white that defies my venomous hiss, the way I claw at the walls.

Her aloofness is both beautiful and enraging. Her white skin, her dark hair, her deep eyes – they mock me as they pick their way around the dissolving apartment, the melting hallways. If only she showed me that she cared, that it mattered to her. If only she would show hurt or pain or anger, then I would know I matter to her. That all *this* – matters.

But she remains passive. She remains unattached to it, to me. I am frustration, I am fury, I am churning heat of morbid jealous sick. I want her in ways only animals dream of. I want to sink all my rage into her, to make her see me.

Now in those moments I recoil from myself. I spend days in the bathroom staring at my own face in the mirror. Spit furious red-black at myself. Break knuckles on cold porcelain. I wash my hands red in bleach and soap, scrub myself raw in the shower. I thrash and spin in those days. I drift and I fade.

And when I lie exhausted on the floor, I hear her soft footsteps padding around the hallways outside. Hear her gentle voice singing like a bird at dawn, warm orange sky.

My tears drip now, falling to the dust on the floor. I smell the rank acidic burning as they eat their way through the wooden boards.

This isn't me. This isn't who I am. I say those words to that face in the mirror. Tell it who I am. I know my face, the lines and angles. That pale geometry that looks back at me, that is a face unknown. Two eyes and a mouth, they are just holes. They curl in shapes of hate, they spit words back at me and laugh. They use words I can barely stand to listen to, even as I feel them leave my own lips. My tongue moves awkwardly around those vowels, leeringly. I make sweating signs with troubled hands, leaning against fading walls. The yellow light sears hot as the sun.

I am losing. This battle, this fight, my struggle. The colour of my skin is fading, I am becoming translucent. My hair is greying, my eyes losing brightness. The poison in this place, in the carpet and furniture, it is seeping into me now, making me sick and washed through. I leak a putrid black ink from my fingers. I lie on the floor and I leak. I lie there and I weep. I twist and I curl, thrash against the walls. She doesn't see. She doesn't see me. She leaves and closes the door. She doesn't care.

In the dark I fill my mouth with her clothing. I stuff it down and choke. I stuff it down and hope. I hope that the filth within me is soaked up. Or that she will return to find me dead and cold.

Those nights, I can't sleep. I sit in the darkness and watch her breathe, watch her dark lips and her chest rise and fall. My thoughts sink into blackness and become just as terrible. I feel them push up in my throat, an inky vomit I choke back and swallow. It rests hard in my breast, pressing against my ribs, forcing air from my lungs. I breathe dust in those night moments, clotted lumps of dry plaster. I breathe shame and fight hard to keep those terrible words down.

I sit amongst the rotting furniture, in the pools of orange light and city sound. I watch television shows about serial killers, unsolved mysteries and alien abductions – the insomniac's smorgasbord. The walls close in, a yellowing box getting smaller and smaller; I close my eyes to the flush of amber from outside.

My world is getting smaller. Everything is shrinking in and collapsing around me. The apartment used to feel too big, like we were rattling around in here. Now I feel claustrophobic; everything is too close. Sometimes I find it hard to breathe and I have to throw open all the windows, desperate for air and space.

How did I get this way? I ask the grainy black and white image of Ted Bundy on the television.

She was angelic when we met. Alabaster white, her hair had the scent of autumn, sweet leaves browning in the low sun. She made me feel safe, whole, real. For a time.

Now I push her away and I throw myself into fits of rage, into seizures of frantic anger, vile jealous words sputtering in choking engine noises. She turns away now, her eyes downcast.

She was angelic when we met. Angelic she remains. I degrade. I waste away into poison. I disintegrate into the carpet. To become nothing more than numb nylon, that is my goal now. She will go on without me, as she always has. I am just a shadow to her. I haunt her life, a ghost of myself.

She doesn't believe in ghosts. I must be some

kind of shade to her, a curious shadow that moves like a visual tick through her life. Sometimes I think that if I shout loud enough, if I make enough noise, then she will hear me, and remember who I am.

And so I shout and I scream at her. I throw things and I beat my chest. I push all my frustration into those outbursts. And I feel a little less like myself after. The way I feel after sex, the wound she never could heal. I get to see her walk away, walk and leave, as I hide myself beneath carpet and wish myself into an emptiness.

I need her to see me, I tell Dennis Rader, as he is led handcuffed into the courtroom.

I watch her from windows, wondering where she is going. She walks with purpose, direction, so different to my own stumbling gait. I draw two eyes in the glass and look through, following her until she is out of my sight. My head leans on the cold glass, eyes closing now. These moments I can't control.

This is how the air gets thin, how time slows and stagnates, how my existence seems to cease. This is how my fists clench and my teeth set at angles, how that snotty black dripping from my nose. This is how those old familiar questions run through my head. Where? Who?

Why? What? How my hands grip the hot metal of the radiator, burning my palms, hoping it will burn away that web of paranoia. Fire to purge the disease. This is how I feel it surging in my veins, how I want to break something. This is how I smell melting polyester, the pungent stench of ozone. This is surely how I die.

I will make her see me again. I will force myself into her vision again. She will see and hear me, like before. And her calming eyes will neutralise this poison, cure my sickness. She will make me whole again, with her.

And if she doesn't want me back? If she continues to look through me as though I am mist?

That question hangs awkwardly. I run my hands under the cold water, soothing the burn, head against the mirror. I look up at the pale ghost. Now there is a cruelty there. It is in the angle of the eyes, the turn on the lips. An unsettling change I wasn't aware of. These things I am not capable of. These things are not of me, yet they are there in the lines of my face, the shadows now that play over me.

I will chew carpet tonight. I will suck it down into my belly and hope it makes me numb. Hope it numbs that cruel voice that whispers.

Now I begin to see that the poison in the apartment is growing into a fine fur, a mold with a faint blue colouring. I see it at first along the skirting: a very fine dark line through all rooms. When I touch it my fingers come away slightly wet. The smell is metallic; it leaves a sharp taste on the tongue.

Through days, the smell gets worse. Strongest in the bedroom where we sleep, together but alone. On my side of the bed it grows thickest, a furry carpet in blue that climbs the walls from the floor. The stench here is the most potent. I can't sleep at night because of the smell. It lingers long in my throat, catches there like battery acid. I try to wash the taste out. I stand in the bathroom gargling and spitting blue-tinged water into the sink. But that scratch remains.

She doesn't notice it. She doesn't see it. She is getting further away from me, more distant. I shout at her as she walks away from me through empty corridors, through doors. She doesn't hear my anger.

I'm sure I can hear it growing. Feel it pushing through the grain in the wood. Through the porous plaster walls. Sitting in the midnight glow of television, I don't hear the muted conversations of twenty-four hour news, but the urgent stretching, the gentle twisting of the whole building. I start to feel it through my whole body. Each day my bones ache and my lungs sag. I seem to struggle for air. As I watch her leave in the morning, I cry that she doesn't see my pain. I claw at the windows, but she doesn't look up. She abandons me to the long hours alone with my agony and poison walls, to the questions I ask myself. The twisted thoughts, the twisting walls.

Through the bedroom the mold spreads and grows, over the floor on one side of the bed. It climbs up the walls and around the window. It creeps now like a web over the glass itself, like fine black fractures. It will soon darken my entire side of the room with blue-black bruise. The stench now is harsher; I can barely breathe in the room. Objects feel further away than they are when I suck on that rank odour. The blood rushes out of my head. It makes me gag; I retch up in the sink, gasping.

I can hear it moving. Hours of day crawl and I lie in rooms listening to it slipping, sliding. The walls and floor, the ceiling, I feel them stretching and moving as the oozing substance pushes through cracks. Pushes through holes. I can feel it filling the wall cavities. I turn on the taps in the bathroom and the water pours out dirty blue and black. It smells, tastes, the same. Sometimes there are pops and groans as some part of the apartment gives in and allows it through. Sags and relaxes.

I kick at the walls. In rage I put my fists through the thin plaster. It explodes in my face in clouds of dust and blue oozing mold. In the bedroom I make a hole in the wall. I roar as the plaster crumbles in my hands and that blue-black mass sloughs to the floor. A slick sick carpet now grows out over nylon. I hear it sigh as it seems to slide in slow motion from the wall cavity, around my ankles. It is so very cold. I begin to feel it numbing me.

She will notice. She must notice this. The mess. The wreck of room, with innards spilled out over the floor, viscera squirming around my feet. I can't let her see this. This is my poison, my sickness, and she can't know how this came to be. I want her to see me, not this; not my guilt and rage.

But it numbs. It cools and soothes like the nylon never did. Like her clothing, chewed on and soft, never did.

I feel the tingling, numbing of that soft ooze creep up from my ankles, through my legs. It gets less intense as my body, burning with the heat of anger, absorbs it. It dissipates through my organs, but I feel its shadow there, settling inside me.

So now I kneel amongst my sins and welcome them back. I scoop them up in my hands and slurp them down into my stomach, hungrily, greedily. Those blue-black crimes make me shudder and groan. I writhe on the floor. Twitch and shake. That softness dissolves in my warm throat, releasing its cold to spread through my flesh. In sick yellow light I make blue my soul. In sick yellow I numb and become hollow.

A calm comes over me. With the cold and the hollow, I feel able to breathe. I can think through the cloud. Kneeling there, amongst the slime of mold, my sickness has created a cure. Somehow. No neon arcs cut through the window to blind me. I feel at ease.

I must make clean these rooms. All disease and mold, this mess must be removed. I cannot allow her to see the ruin of my sickness, the stain on the walls, the great blubber that spills into the room. I know she will see me now. This blue-black cleanses me of the dirt inside. I feel hollow but my body feels whole. I am numb inside, but feel more than I ever did.

Now these innards of wall fill black sacks, the poured-out plasterboard and sick. They stack inside the cavities, a secret hidden. Like bodies they pile, reeking shame. Later at night, when she sleeps, when I lie awake, I will take them and bury them. While she sleeps, I will dig deep and dump my guilt in the black earth. Down it will churn, rot and leak. The worms and beetles it will feed. Out of sight.

I know now the apartment is fighting the poison. It is resisting. The mold is a counter-measure, it is antibodies. I breathe in and feel the apartment breathe with me. Its concrete lungs swell. It feels clearer as I feel clearer. Air moves through these halls and rooms, moves dust from the television screen and the smell of her perfume from the bedroom. These walls made me well, as I made them sick. Together we will recover, concrete and flesh, our salvation tied to one another.

She walks through the door, a silhouette moving smoothly through pale light. Now she looks up at me and her smile is bright and vibrant. The colour of the room drains away to monochrome, leaving only her smile, a deep and pulsing red.

We make love in blue light. Our bodies move together urgently, her softness and sweet aroma like it used to be. Her hair always had that smell of her work, the sterile air of the office, of piles of paper and false daylight. Then deeper, the bleach and chemicals.

We lie together under thin sheets, wrapped in

each other. I hear her voice whispering, but I can't really make out the words. She may not be using real ones. She used to do that when she was happy. Sometimes when she was sad. I would often lie in bed listening to her in the shower, singing songs with no words, her melodies drifting. She made it all soft.

Now she feels distant. I feel her heat next to me, but her voice is beneath an ocean, a turbulent, grey expanse. I am below those terrible waves, sinking.

In the morning, the air cool through the apartment. I hear her showering, but I can't move. I lie paralysed on the bed, a tangle of sheets and my own limp body. She comes back into the room and gets dressed, her white uniform crisp and fresh in the early morning light. She doesn't look at me as she dresses, and I feel the skin across my back tighten like plastic under a heat lamp.

She doesn't see me.

And now I feel it in my groin, in my heart. Feel that burn coursing through me. And I see the way she walks, the movement of her hips, the curve of her shape. Her heels. Her lips. Her scent crawls from the bed like spiders into my skull. I see now how she talks. Feel her betrayals like jagged shards of broken glass, each one thrust into me. Each day she leaves, each day I watch another abandonment. Each day now this torrent of rage grows and now it festers in the walls, a fungus feeding on the vibrations of my skull, the fire in my blood. This blue-black ink that I spit in the mirror each day, this is the shit this mold grows fat on.

Now I see this is no cure, this is concentrated poison, my own hate filtered through brick and plaster, through the prism of my own confinement. These four enclosed walls, I bang around in them. I fall and I twist in the light of a swinging bulb; lunatic shadows dance. I sucked down on the fat of my own anger. What damage I have done.

Movement returns to my limbs slowly over hours, over painfully slow hours while the day leaks away and blue-tinged tears drip to the pillow.

I grab the bags from the wall cavity. They leak and ooze across the floor, a blue-black trail in my wake. It occurs to me that maybe the mold had always been there, growing silently in the walls, under the floor. Perhaps I became infected by some spores, drank polluted water. If I can clean the apartment, maybe I will be well again.

I drag those bags into the small patch of enclosed garden at the rear of the building. I dig through the grass, down into the damp earth, my hands clawing. Nails cracked and broken, a hole opens up into the ground. I wonder about burying myself; that would solve a lot of problems. The bags fall down to the bottom with a squelch like a corpse. Wiping bluish sweat from my eyes, I push the earth over those bags. I seal them down in the bowels of ground. Under the grass, under the sky, they will rot and disintegrate into worms.

Now I throw bleach into the apartment. Through the rooms and the halls, chemical cleansers run, the stink making me choke. I scrub the walls, the floor, on my knees with knuckles bloodied and broken. My hands become red in that caustic wash as I scrape the mold from the walls – a blunted knife, a hatchet, my fingers. Through the door it empties from the apartment, blue-black effluent, clotted with lumps of furred plaster. Inky blood it pools in the outside hallway.

It is streaked in red now, as my hands bleed into the filthy bleach-water that I sweep with an old broom through the apartment, out into the hall. My hands blister and peel from the chemical scald, the ruin of this shame.

This is how she smells when she returns to

me. She leaves in a cloud of scent and returns with the stain of chemicals on her skin, in her hair. It used to make me recoil from her, but in time I grew used to it, and as my sickness grew, I learned to want it, as I wanted her. The clinging black stain on the back of her neck, her hair in my face, breathing it in down into my lungs, deep into me. Her breath heavy. Her lips so red.

I knew it made her feel bad. She was ashamed of that canker. I would see her scrubbing herself in the shower, her pale body raw as she tried to erase that stench from her skin. Of soaps and moisturisers, her skin would taste, but the metallic itch would still sting the back of my throat. I would watch her cry at night and wonder what pain that perfume hid.

I know I won't be able to mask the smell of bleach in the apartment. She will notice it when she returns. And she will feel haunted. I know I will watch her in the shower, dreaming of drowning, and guilt will well up through me like an old weeping sore.

I think of burning the furniture. The bedding. Her clothes. Perhaps I should burn down the apartment. We could leave this place and begin again elsewhere. Somewhere clean. Somewhere safe.

But I couldn't be sure the disease would remain with the ashes. It is in me. I am the seed of this sickness. My core burns with it. So here we must remain, and I must find a way through it. Find a path, an escape route. One both of us can follow.

*

Through days and the mold does not return. Yellow are the walls, nylon is the carpet; we sleep together in the bedroom. It has been a week and she has not talked about the poison-soaked apartment we used to inhabit. I am feeling whole. There is shape and definition to my features. I no longer look in the mirror and see through me.

But she does not sleep well. She thrashes in the bed at night, tangles herself in the sheets and wakes up shrieking, her body glistening with sweat. She says that something is growing. Something terrible. It is inside her, she says, she can feel it pushing to exist, trying to claw its way out of her. We talk of pregnancy, the fear of another life. It drives her to panic, she cries for hours alone, black tears down her white face in the bedroom, while I pace, while I wait, while I do nothing.

During the night I watch over her from the chair next to the bed. Cold in the stark neon light of city, breathing with its traffic noises and alarms. A stuttering, frantic soundtrack that defines silence for us in these days. I sit and I wait for her nightmares to take hold of her, so I can be there to protect her, prevent her throwing herself around the room.

That first night, in our apartment halls she twisted and danced, violent in sick yellow light, her shadows ghosted against the walls in shapes of other people. Her screams were strangulated, caught in concrete. I chased her down, legs tangled in themselves, but she fought back, raged in my arms. Scratched and clawed, she spat acid and arcs of light, her pores bled with the sulphurous neon of bad city street lighting.

Her whole body stiffened, caught in a seizure, eyes rolling back, dead like. Panic struck me, through tears I called her name, shook her. Her skin went from pale white to grey. Her chest didn't move. Red lips became dry and black. And time stretched achingly long.

When it was over she slid into a deep sleep that lasted hours. I paced the bedside, the hall, I stared long into the bathroom mirror. I asked it questions. I hunted through the walls, peering into the cracks, sniffing at the windows. I checked my spit for discolouration.

When she awoke, she told me about the thing growing inside her. All arms and bleeding. A raging furious something. A blur of violence. We cried together. We cried tears clear.

It is all my fault. I brought a sickness into this place, and now she is riven with it.

The fits go on, each night. I wrap her in blankets as she rolls on the floor. Wrap her in me as she tears at the air, barks at the shadows, her face flushed in amber. Her cries slap against the walls and return to me a distorted, animal wailing, but flat, made unreal. In these moments she seems skewed from herself, fractured in space. A look, a sound, a smell. Something feels different.

As I struggle with her back to the bedroom, I think: I don't recognise this woman.

I am living with a stranger. Or maybe a ghost. A screaming phantom haunts me at night, dragging me from the bed, her screeching that of a banshee, a terrifying howl that cuts me to the core. I feel blood run from my nose when she flickers through walls. She throws books at me from other rooms, as I run for cover behind furniture. In the mornings I am sure I hear the shower, and I think of that shifting figure, but when I look there I see nothing. The sound follows me when I leave.

Every night, those jump-cuts in shafts of yellow light, her image a broken film, her voice a fragmented soundtrack, screaming from somewhere far away. So much interference. So much static. It hisses while I sleep. I sense a great anger in the apartment, a rage boiling like at the centre of a sun. Feel it growing in intensity every day; a great pressure swelling. I think of it collapsing into itself, becoming a nightmarish singularity. I exist on its event horizon, feeling the pull of its gravity, feeling my body stretching interminably towards that great black maw.

For a moment I remember a face.

I wonder what I have done to deserve this haunting. I pace the apartment in the wake of her raging, the trail of trauma cutting a path of polyester poison along the ceiling. It drips and hisses as it eats through the carpet. I feel radiated. Her ultra-violet eyes burn through brick, through my bone. I am left with reddened skin and searing eyes.

I feel guilty, but don't know why. I have forgotten something. I lie on the floor, the ceiling spinning around in arcs of stained yellow. In the back of my mind there is a patch of dark, of empty. Nothing. Something used to be there. Memories, history. My time. Now it has gone. I can smell something sharp and metallic when I think too long about it. An itch at the back of my throat makes me vomit and I feel hollow inside.

In the bathroom my sick colours the water black and blue, bruised through by an emptiness. I spit ink at the mirror, beading the same darkness in sweat and tears. I hear the screaming of that shade, my ghost, surging in the bedroom behind me. Growing and growing as I empty myself in streaks of increasing red and blue, blood and bile. I feel those x-ray eyes scanning, the shower running, my own cries.

The walls shudder and light fittings swing as if in an earthquake. I can feel the walls swelling, beginning to crack with pressure. Something is leaking through those cracks. I can smell it.

The air begins to fill with dust and rage and her thrashing in the doorway, terrible in her burning. In her blinding fire.

Something is growing. Something is pushing. Something is yearning to become.

LIFE

IS

LOST

IN

THIS

HELL

There is a tree in the yard. In the patch of green walled in by grey, the light overhead orange and blistering, a false sun for that young sapling. I can see it from the bedroom window, small and bare, the size of a young child, its short leafless limbs hang pathetically by its side.

I sit and watch it grow, staring down from the window. Daylight fades to darkness and the square of garden is bleached in amber. It feeds on that sodium lighting, sucks its cold energy into those thin branches. Nothing else lives there. Nothing else grows but the ragged green of grass and the rats that scurry between shadows.

Night bleeds through to morning, and I feel

the tree stretch. It provokes a yawn from me, a shifting of air through the apartment.

I go down to the yard. The tree stands waist high. Tiny buds form lumps along its branches, the arms of a child riddled with cancerous tumours. They look like sores, rising, ready to burst and leak. The trunk is as thick as my own arm, bony, a silver-grey, with a hint of blue when the sunlight catches it. Around the base I notice some ripped pieces of black plastic sack, as if the tree has torn through them in its effort to reach the light of the sun, to break the earth and live.

The shape of the tree against the sky is as a gnarled hand, fingers stretching. I sit for a few moments and stare at that deformed silhouette until my eyes burn. Black on blue, a contorted puzzle cut from paper, I see those fingers curl to a fist, clenched and strong against a sky going grey. I make a fist of my own and hold it up next to that of the tree. My pale hand trembles, knuckles show through white, so white I think about them breaking the skin. I doubt that would even hurt, so dry and thin my body is.

The appearance of the tree marks a change in the behaviour of my ghost. She no longer torments me these nights. Instead I see her twisting around it, her jarring, broken image cutting in and out of the darkness, through strobing light, a visual static hiss. Rather than her terrible wailing, she sings a wordless song, a hymn that makes my teeth chatter and the wallpaper peel. The lamp light flickers, dims.

I can't tell if she is feeding the tree, or if it is drawing on her. She seems to be waiting for something to happen, maybe for it to grow more. I measure it each morning, mark its height on the wall by the window. Its progress is slow but steady, a daily increase, its limbs getting longer, stronger, its trunk taller, thicker, the bark darker. Her song too grows more intense, louder. When she sings I have to cover my ears, and I feel the vibrations all through the apartment. And the smell, a choking stench emanates from somewhere within the building, filling the rooms. I open windows to try and let in the air, but it is still. I throw them wide open, hang half outside so I can breathe, but I find my lungs filling with that rank itch that makes me gag and retch in the bathroom, cold light on my shoulders, mirror streaked.

When I sleep, it is with the warmth of the sun on my body. These days are long and humid, the air thick and heavy. I dream of a woman I think I used to know. She is beautiful, but sad. A monochrome figure in a world of vibrant colour, only her lips searing through red. She talks to me, but no sound comes from that mouth, only a torrent of blue liquid. It pours like water from her, dark as ink, impenetrable. Her hands move in slow arcs to stem the flood; her figure shifts, blurs. Her edges lose definition and she melts away, a bloody handkerchief in a sink of cold water.

Sometimes I'm following her through arterial corridors, great hospital hallways that stretch out over a barren landscape, a dark field, flat, featureless. The walls are all marbled blue and black. The concrete is dry and it flakes away, corroded flesh, as the plaster skin crumbles and falls to the ground. Those blue-black veins leak, a kind of puss weeps out, oozing down the walls. The building bleeds, weeps tears thick as sludge.

Each day when I measure the tree, I leave notes for my ghost. I scrawl them in pencil on pieces of wallpaper torn from the bedroom. I ask her where she is from. Who she is. Why she comes at night. What does she want. Perhaps the dreams are her way of answering. I don't know. I keep measuring the tree, and each day it is a little taller, a little thicker. And the hollowness inside me is a little greater, spreading.

There is an aroma that comes from the tree, like spring blossom only sickly and metallic.

It reminds me of the stench that comes when my ghost sings at night. It is there as invisible clouds when I go down to measure and leave my notes. I walk into that haze and cough. My hand to my mouth and nose. Sometimes I think I am going to be sick.

I tuck my wallpaper notes into the black sacks that erupt from the ground around the base of the tree trunk. The dirty plastic flaps, like thick animal skin, hide a dark, foul-smelling waste. I never investigate that rot; the stench around the tree seems to emanate from there. The notes are folded carefully and slid under those skin flaps. Many now bulge there, and as the tree grows the space gets smaller, so they are pushed out onto the grass. Some have blown away, carried on the wind away from here.

I write my notes and I record the tree's measurements on the wall I tear the paper from. I use the same pencil to do both. It is wearing down, getting smaller. There are pencil shavings all over the bedroom floor. They curl in the sun like dried, flaking skin, and for moments I stare at my hands as if I am peeling.

Now the water begins to run dirty brown, and smells of damp leaves, the decomposing autumn. Through the taps it runs. It drips now all night, a rivulet of burnt orange trailing down the sink, pooling in the bath tub. It makes me think of my childhood, running through forests, chasing; of abandoned ruins in the trees. Those days of low sun, of grey sky, heavy, they hang in the apartment now. I feel a chill through my bones when I touch the walls, the encroaching winter, the warning of. I think I feel the gentle fall of orange, of leaves, of trees shedding.

The wallpaper skin of the apartment is damp through and peeling off all over. Beneath, in the plaster and the brick, I can see thin brown veins spreading. Here and there, some break through. They are tree roots, fine and young, pushing through the walls. I see them through the ceiling, and now in the floor, jutting up between the boards, forcing their way through the carpet.

From the windows I watch, and the tree watches me. As it grows, pushes itself through the apartment, reaching. I will not touch those roots. I step over them, a child avoiding cracks in the pavement. Yet it wants me to. I sense a yearning in that bark and wood. I will not drink the water from those taps, not that polluted dark filth. I will not let that inside me.

So I am wasting away now. I am drinking rain water and eating wallpaper scraps. It makes me sick, but the void inside me spreads with each day, and it is only a matter of time before I am nothing.

I imagine being nothing when I try to sleep. When I lie and listen to her singing at night, watching roots twisting across the ceiling. I try to imagine being a void, an absence of matter. But the tree is insistent and continues to push in, as she pushes in with her song. I open my eyes, and the four walls close in around me, my focus lost. My search for an emptiness lost. And as I lie there, small cracks being to appear in the ceiling.

Through those cracks the smell of damp wood seeps. The stench of oozing dirt and filth. Of the cold wet soil and decomposition. It descends over me as a very fine mist. It makes everything glisten with wetness, as though the apartment is in a sweat. This mist spreads through the rooms and halls, fills all the space. Pushing out all the air. All I can breathe now is the dank rot of tree, sucking it into my lungs, taking it into my blood stream.

I am becoming polluted, my blood changing from red to a dirty brown. My spit and tears carry that taint already. I stand in the bathroom with a knife held over my wrist. If I cut, my blood will pour as river water into the bath.

I stare at myself in the mirror, naked and

wasted. The blade catches yellow light and arcs in my eyes. My image ghosts, a broken signal.

The dampness spreads, gets worse. Water drips now from the ceiling, a dirty brown liquid that pools in places. I think about tasting it. I feel my body crave it. All around, growing roots bursting, and puddles of water reflecting. This would sustain me if I were to eat it, if I were to drink that discoloured liquid.

But I know this will not save me. I know this will only fill me with poison and waste, with the rot of dying trees, of foliage becoming mulch, liquefying. I would disintegrate into worms and feed the tree outside.

So now I know that this apartment is dying. It is riddled with so many roots, the reaching tendrils of the tree. It is a parasitic infection, sucking all the life from the apartment, from me. As the tree gains height and girth, the apartment fades and crumbles. In turn I am blurring, becoming indistinct. Phasing in and out. When I see my reflection, it stutters, jump-cuts. I don't see my own shadow any more.

Now the tree roots grow so thick and numerous that the apartment door is no longer there. They cover the walls, bursting through the plaster to invade the space. I have stopped measuring the tree. I can no longer leave this place. Trapped, I wait to be crushed down to a single point. To be embraced by those coiling limbs.

I continue writing notes to my ghost, although now they are on the sheets of the bed, on my hands and my legs. I sleep wrapped in my words, my questions, hoping they will bleed into me, that the ink will sink into me and she will answer me in my dreams.

Her answers do not come. I only find myself wandering those forests, the ground a thick carpet of red-brown. There are trees and bushes with small bright red berries. When I reach out to them everything sinks into a soft focus and the colour melts away. Nothing but the red.

I get lost in those monochrome woods. Amongst those terrible trees, their arms reaching to grab me. I know I am getting lost here.

And those red berries everywhere, but always unreachable. Always blurring away as my hand stretches, closes to grab them. It all goes red, blood seeping into my eyes. I thrash around, sightless in those trees.

I lie on the bed, drifting, shifting, becoming less real. My perception of time has vanished.

I no longer know if I have been here days, months or years. It could even be hours. I hold my hands to my eyes. I can see through them, see the bone and the network of veins pumping my dark blood. When I lower them, I see the twisting root system of the tree, a mass of curling brown, like the flowing hair of. Someone. There are no more walls, no more ceiling or floor, just the tangled rhizomes, fibrous. Those shoots are thick and strong now; I know the tree outside is tall and mighty. I would be able to see it through the window, if it were still there.

This can no longer be called an apartment. It is a subterranean cavern, dank and dark. A dull blue light ebbs from within the web of roots. It is warm and humid here, everything is damp to touch. For a few moments I think about mold growing.

There are no longer rooms or hallways here. Now they are hollow chambers and passages, as though carved from rock and now overgrown. Gone are the square edges and corners, here are curves and twists, coiling tentacle shapes that dangle. All that remains that was this apartment has gone. All but me and the bed I lie on. I think about why the roots haven't consumed me yet. There is a gap of a few inches around the bed through which I can still see some flooring, as though they can come that close and no more.

I wrap myself in bed sheets, in sheets covered in my begging notes to my ghost who never answers, who never responds or acknowledges. I bury myself deep amongst those words and the soft bedding, curling up and hiding. Curling up and hoping the numbing blankness will come for me.

I sob quietly in my word-sheet cocoon. My tears soak into the covers and the ink runs, begins to leach out of the material, seeping into my body. That cold blue courses through my veins now. Sensing every word I ever wrote sink deep into my muscles, into the fat of my being. I pull the covers tighter around me, wanting to choke, suffocate, to drown in my words.

And I feel myself sinking. I feel myself as if swallowed by something huge. With a cry caught in my throat I try to scramble free of the bedding, but suddenly I am falling, and it is too late now.

I move through the slick wet body of this tree, through its root system, its veins, its arterial branches. I descend into black organs where blue liquid thick with the reek of decomposition pools, coils in currents. I slide and I slip, born through soft plant openings, through mouths, toothless rents into caverns of twisting blue light and indigo arcs. Branches hold and embrace me, then push me and pull me, the touch of the wood soft then hard then urgent. They support then bend, bowing to let me fall, to slip away down some other throat. I feel that sap on my lips, in my mouth, oozes down my throat, so thick and sweet, it fills me up, makes me heavy. It gums up my nose and my eyes. I cough and choke on its cloying viscous; that succulent drip of thick.

I fall further down, through dark and through sap, my lungs full. Then brilliant light, white and yellow, in halos, artefacts of blue fracture my vision. I am pushed through, out, through the dark and the sap and the roots that tangle. I roll out into warm light and soft; I cough and vomit. On my hands and knees I empty myself, a torrent of blue-black vileness drips from my nose, pours from my mouth, up through my throat. I choke it up from my lungs and fill them with the air. Take my first breath, ragged and broken.

My eyes struggle to adjust. They sting and stream with tears. All shapes swim in colour and blur together. I can't make out edges.

Now I hear a woman's voice. It sounds familiar, like I know her, but in my daze it is slightly distorted, like I am underwater and she is calling to me beneath the waves. She tells me not to be afraid. Her words are calming; they soothe away the panic and confusion. I feel a warmth swelling inside me, a kind of elation, joy. I am suddenly smiling because my ghost is talking to me. Finally she is answering.

Soft and sweet, she presses something to my lips. Eat, she says, and I do as she tells me, chewing and swallowing the succulent fruit. I feel it deep within me, pushing the hollowness aside. My vision sharpens a little; some details become defined, but she remains a grainy image, a shape of fog and neon.

Sleep now, she tells me, and I close my eyes, feeling warm, with a fullness inside me that feels good. I hear her humming quietly close to me, yet somehow still very far away. Her tune drifts further as I fall into sleep, into arms, branches covered in vibrant green leaves that catch and hold me.

Now the apartment is a field; now a tree; now a chamber of soft, swirling blue. I sleep and I grow here, I wake and eat the sweet fruit she collects from the tree, that blooms on its sprawling branches. Those berries embrace me as arms, long and tender, snaking through my body, spreading warmth. She takes them each day, from high limbs and low, she climbs through that maze of leaf, returning to me.

Returning to me.

Her voice continues to remind me of someone, but I can never remember who. Deep within me the itch of recognition claws and aches. She hushes my questions and brings me more fruits.

She leaves me at night, alone and weary, drained somehow, too faded to move. My strength is yet to return, is what she tells me, so I must rest. I must recover. From what, I don't know. Everything is fuzzy, my memory a sluggish river, thick with fat. There are things I know I must recall, faces and places, things I have done.

But it is all muddy, those waters polluted with dirt, grit, an effluent my mind is leaking, like a bleeding wound. I try to plot points in my mind, of things I know, the solid moments. Then my focus is lost, it begins to blur and degrade, then is gone.

When she is with me during the day, she sings songs to me as she brings me fruit. Her mouth moves in slow motion and her words seem to slur into one another, becoming a single sound, shifting in frequency and tone. She is monochrome made, phasing shades of grey, she ghosts through. Sometimes she seems to flicker before my eyes, like bad lighting, a candle. A nervous twitch. Her eyes never blink when she looks at me, and under her gaze I feel like a child.

Now the apartment is a hospital, and she moves through walls as the angel nurse, the saviour of patients. She takes away sickness and eats up the cancers. Her song follows her through halls long and dark. Lights flash in a Morse code as she passes. When she is out of sight, her hymn still lingers, reverberating from walls.

I sleep then. Out of sight, I sleep.

But sleep is abrupt in these long halls of shadow. She returns more and more, perched by my bedside in yellow lamp-light, her hands full of the blue fruits. Eat, she says, pushing those bulbous sacks of sweet to my lips.

And I eat because she tells me to, because she tells me this is good for me. The sweetness fills me, but she never appears to be more than a grey blur, a smudge in my vision. I try to ask why, when will I be able to see her? But she just tells me to eat more, to sleep, to not worry. She will look after me.

And I have no reason to doubt her, to not trust what she tells me. Except that days and days in this room pass, curtains drawn to the light outside, and I feel an urgency in my flesh, an anxiety that itches.

She comes to me now, and for the first time I resist, refuse, I turn my head away, smelling bleach in the pillow.

There is moment when I see smooth thighs, pale and white, parting.

This will make you well, she says, in a waterfall of words. She turns my head towards her, thin delicate fingers gentle on my face.

Her lips burn black, then blue, and I smell something metallic. I cough as my throat goes dry, itches. She hushes me like a mother and those berries pass my lips, each bursting in my mouth, releasing juicy flesh dripping. There, she says with a smile, take your medicine.

The anxiousness grows worse with each dose of blue fruit, each burst of berry juice makes that internal tremble more severe. When she leaves I hold up my hands and watch them shake uncontrollably. My mouth feels dry and my legs weak. I begin to cry for her.

My medicine, it becomes my addiction now. I am becoming dependent on that fruit, on that blue nectar she brings to me. Without, I am torn apart by cramp, riven with pains that radiate from my stomach, through my crotch. I sweat, soaking through my bedclothes, through my sheets. I wail and whimper through the nights, while she tends to others, those other patients in other rooms off of other halls. She sees to their needs while I suffer, while I thrash in agony. Can she not hear my cries? Can she not feel my rage when she finally comes to me in the light of a piss-weak sun?

I greet her then with sullen silence. I spit the fruit seeds on the floor, dribble, drizzle, drool that sweet meat down my chin. As a child.

She ignores my petulance. She continues to hum, to sing her songs. Those melodies calm me through the days, and my sweating aches dissipate. I listen to her, watch her move around the room, floating. She straightens the thin curtains that cover the windows. I want her to lie with me, to love me, painfully, angrily, to destroy me. My desire for her, my need for her, increases with my dependency.

She asks if I would like to see the view from the window, to see the garden, the sky. I can only look at her, that shimmering shape of her, standing by the window. I can only sense a smile on her face, and I know I am now crying because I need her so much, and my body is riven with desire, the ache of an addiction that only she can satiate.

That pause in time lasts for what feels like an eternity. And when she opens the curtains, there is a roaring like that of a waterfall, a great torrent that rushes. My hands cover my ears, but I still hear it. Still feel it like a violent wave through my body.

A cold light now from a sliver of sky I can see through the broken, black branches of a tree, an angular shape that twists in the square of window. See those blue fruits growing there. See them bud and glow. A leafless ragged scratch of tree, my body reacts violently.

Blue-black vomit spews from my mouth, splatters across the floor and spreads in a thick clotted pool. I moan now as my body twists in pain. Turn away from the window, my back to that tree. I sigh and make fists, fingers curling tight.

I hear her clean up behind me. Feel her fingers in my hair. Feel her push soft fruit to my lips.

She leaves me now, as dusk creeps into the day. She leaves me staring out of the window at the large tree in the courtyard, a patch of green walled in by grey. And I think of that tree ablaze. I think of it burning and crumbling to cinders, ash piling up in the small square of green. I see those fruits burst in bright blue clouds, the sweet juice sizzling in the heat.

I think of a fire so intense the window glass between me and it melts and my skin shrinks, tightens. My hair smoulders and my eyes burst. I think of a fire that would burn and rage and twist as a storm through this building, across the field, and reduce all to blackened crust.

Then this afternoon, this hollow afternoon riddled with sweat-thrashing and throat hoarse with shouts. Alone, no one comes. No sweet soft. No tender flesh oozing with blue berry juices.

With tears stinging my face, I turn towards the pale afternoon, towards the courtyard and the tree, towards my hope of fire and rage.

There she sits, beneath that tree, under its spreading arms. She is reading from small folded pages. She holds a large bundle of them in her hands; many more are scattered on the ground around her. I think she might be smiling, but she may also be weeping, as her hand goes to her face as if to wipe her cheeks.

My blood churns as acid. I spit poison to the floor in a thick burning glob of blue-black filth. I hiss, throw myself to the walls. These betrayals, these treacheries, they clot up my veins as fat, cling to my throat, stone artefacts coughed up, choked on. I suffer while she attends to secret notes, admirers and lovers. I wrench alone, twist in this sweat-soaked bed for her. And she doesn't see.

And days pass, and nights follow, alone in my room, alone in my bed, cursing, coursing black blood through pores, breathing the dust in the air and forming angles with my body, joints aching in the dark. I make shapes, a code of limbs, symbolic of my pain and fury. I hope to lie paralysed like this. I hope to become stone so that she may find me frozen in my moment of suffering.

I see bodies hanging from the tree. They swing back and forth, in daylight and through the night. Those broken necks and limp expressions stare: three, four, five gently swaying corpses. I wonder if those faces are me. How many faces do I have?

For a time I am the tree. I stand in the courtyard, in a field, on a mountainside, my arms reaching wide. My skin is dry and peeling. I am naked of foliage, nothing grows on me now. Once I dribbled sap, a thick, sweet ooze that fed my strong body, gave life to my leaves. Now it hardens within my trunk, solidifies and calcifies in my limbs.

This dying tree, this useless monolith now rotting. I can only stand there, my roots running deep through the ageless earth, but withered, no longer drawing nutrients. I watch seasons pass, I see the arc of the sun as a blur across the sky.

And I see her below me, sitting against my body. I cannot feel her warmth through my dead bark. I cannot cry for her. She reads notes, small scraps of torn paper, the writing in scrawling pencil. I feel her body shudder, with laughter or sadness I don't know, but the movement shivers through me to the tips of my branches.

Now she stands and walks away. I want to cry out to her, shout to her, call her back to me, into my arms. No voice breaches this wooden form. No sound can be made with my brittle limbs.

As I watch her back disappearing into the fog of field, my husk of bark erupts into a plague of hives. Of pustulating sores. Of weeping blue rents and boils. My wood-skin burns as the blue ooze, this blackening sickness sears through, pushes through, hissing and spitting. It runs in rivulets down the crevasses in my trunk, pooling around my roots. It seeps into the earth. The ground swallows, absorbs. And as she vanishes from sight finally, the field becomes black. This field now ravaged.

On this morning I awake to my fingers

bleeding blue. On this morning I awake to my wallpaper ripped and torn. My nails are broken and chewed down, stained, my lips taste of ink and blood. Around me amongst the bedding are the crumbs of dried out wallpaper, the smudgy marks of inky hands wiped clean.

Under the mattress I discover a pile of notes, scrawled in bloody-blue ink, on sheets of ragged wallpaper. The words are desperate, begging, pleading; they slur across the page in streaks. There is a violence in their shape. They rage on the paper. Was this me? Did I spit out these words?

Now the walls reveal to me what they have hidden. Through the lining paper they bleed, blue blood seeping like through cotton. They appear in huge letters, angry, hateful words, all over the surface of every wall.

And now the ceiling too.

And now the floor.

I taste the ink in my throat. It itches there, harsh, rasping. It seeps from under my fingernails, a dirty blue trace of guilt, a rancorous snot.

The words before me make a shameful stain. I want to hide from them, but they are all over. I close my eyes, but I hear them shouting in my head. I hear her whisper them to me, her mouth, her lips, close to my ear, so close it sends quivers down my spine. I hear the spite in her voice, the hurt. I cannot hide from the things I have done.

My life is lost in this hell. I would put my fist through those walls. I would put a bullet in my own head. Hang myself from the branches of the tree. I would fall and be consumed by this earth, rendered black by my own useless rage, my own failure. I would rot with my anger, spent now. I would return to maggots and worms, blowflies and slime. I would be soil for the grass, blackened by my turmoil, food for the trees. I would rise up through the roots, into the bark, into the sap. I would be fruit growing ripe and sweet on the sprawling shapes of branches, punching like fists into the sky.

# EVERY
# VIOLENT
# EFFIGY

Now these walls close me down. Now I fall to the floor, fall to the ceiling, thrash. Now I cry tears and yell at the brick, I scream at the walls, those words. My fists rage against them. My blood pours, thick. I spin and I jerk, twisting through hours. Over and over I blur and I ghost against yellow walls, sick words shouting in blue shapes.

Now I sag. I lie and weep. I leak. An old sack spilling shit across the floor, I breathe in strangulated gasps.

Years and I am alone here. Years and the cobwebs grow. The dust carpets like snow. The rot, the smell of decay, and those words all around that mock me. I lift my arms. My hands curve in slow arcs across the milky sun that hangs low.

Years and I phase through positions. I lie on the floor, a parody of a dead man. I curl on the bed, asleep but wide awake. I stand against walls, trying to push myself through the brick. Sleepless years in a low amber light, that of dying stars. In soft focus, my vision never quite sharp, never quite focused. I stumble through these years. I fumble and I leave no trace of myself in the dust.

I shudder on the bed, under cold light, the fading of walls at dusk. I wrap myself in arms. I hold myself in hopeless moments.

All these years and yet I still yearn for her. My body still aches and churns, I still weep sweat through thin jaundiced skin. Now I know she has left for good. I will never recover from this sickness, this addiction. She has gone and will never return to me. I have pushed her too far away this time. She has left to cure herself of me, to recover from me. I have never wanted to recover from her. But these years I wonder, was she my disease or was I hers?

So now as sunlight throws shadows long across the room, I lie on the floor and hope soon to disintegrate. I hope soon to be ash. Shadows retreat to darkness and stars emerge, blistering the sky beyond the window with pin points of brilliant white.

All these days I spend wandering the halls and rooms of this abandoned ruin. I have spent weeks hunting for her amongst the dark and the dust. Called her name into corridors long and wrecked, against flat walls that peel paint in strips. No echo returns to me. I hope that she is here somewhere, hiding. I hope to find her again. I hope that in the searching I purge this disease, that she will see how sorry I am for everything.

And there is a faint pulse, a throb from somewhere deep within this pile of stone. It is weak, but is warm and I long for it. It lights up the same parts of me that she made bright and alive. So through the rust and the decay, the rotten body of this concrete, I still move.

This warren of corridors and rooms, they never end. They shift and they turn on themselves. I get lost for days, only to find myself minutes from my room. I sleep in rotting old beds. The mattress stink of damp. And always, somewhere, the faint lines of roots working through the walls, bursting up through the floor, as though pursuing me through this place.

Now I find evidence and signs of her presence, clues to her location or that she has been here.

I fill my pockets with scraps of paper, rags that smell of her hair, wallpaper with strange symbols scrawled across it that seem to suggest a vector of exploration.

All these clues now come with me back to my room. Here I arrange them, I lay them out. I join them up. They form a huge map sprawling now across the floor, moving up one wall. I have found old photographs and papers in abandoned offices, traces of lipstick on mirrors. I stare at the faces in those grainy black and white images. Some of those eyes look like hers; the hair here resembles how she was. They are pinned to the wall, inky lines join them to new clues now recovered, now added and merged in with the rest.

I never look at the tree. I never turn to face it. I hear it though. Sometimes its aging branches tap at the window, trying to draw my attention away from my map. Sometimes I feel its roots growing beneath me, pushing and insinuating. It makes me crawl and clench. Through nights, as I lie sweating, shivering, I know it reaches to me, its long fingers spreading through the room in shadows, ready to wrap around me, to snatch me back into its embrace.

I never look at the tree, but it irradiates me. Through the windows I am blasted day and night with violent, invisible rays. They move through the ultraviolet spectrums, infrared. I am burned and seared, my flesh itches, and through these days I claw at my skin, desperate to peel myself free, as though this body were drying, shrivelling under the hard light gaze of the tree.

I return to the hulk day after day, to the cavernous concrete, this multitude of stone corridors and rooms empty of life, breathing the rot. I write across the walls wherever I find clues and signs of her. I scrawl my name, scratch it into the brick and plaster. If I could, I would burn myself into the very fabric of this place. I hope that my words surge through and seek her out, that she will hear them through the walls and floor, feel their vibrations, their urgency.

Those words I leave through the halls. I follow them now, as a guide, a pathway through all this wreckage. With more papers and photographs, items of clothing, I use my smeared ink scrawl to find my way back to my room, back to the map, where I can work in cold sweat moments, knees bruised and knuckles raw. This sprawling tangle of symbols and signs, it spreads and grows, branches and roots.

And then I stop. A sound floats to me. A distant melody. A song. It comes as a humming, a gentle throb through the stone. I feel it move up my arms and legs. It sinks into my body. Then that sound swells up and I am choked with tears.

My limbs twist with aching desire, my desperate need for her. In my knees an arthritic jarring. My body burns from my crotch to my throat. She calls to me now through the agony of my bones. In my flesh I feel her hymn, a virus spreading, rooted in my organs and muscles. It smells of fresh paint, the chemical streak, the pungent poison of bleach that hangs in the air now.

Awake in my room here, her song in my ears still. I know she is close, I know she is near, but getting further away.

And for the first time I look up at the tree. Through the filth-smeared windows I see that black outline against the sky, like a fracture in space. It seems flat, featureless on that backdrop of grey and bruise-coloured evening.

And I look from the tree to my map, a twisting mess of shapes and lines in ink, with sections branching from a central trunk. The realisation makes me cold inside. I feel myself sinking, as though being swallowed, falling through black, through blue, into a vast nothing. I would feel rage if I did not feel so completely hopeless.

Years and I have not rid myself of the influence of the tree. Years not looking, not seeing, not believing, and I have created my own tree in images, a branching system in shapes of her. All these years of waste, all those miles of wandering, all those clues gathered. That tree continues to infect me, to influence my thoughts. How can there be escape from this? How can I hope to find her when all the routes I flee down end in root and tangle?

I should have known better. I shouldn't have been so stupid as to believe I could actually find her with that thing watching my every move. That trickster, that mocking black.

But she is calling to me now, calling as if screaming out, as though a prisoner. Her cries seem to sear through my map, through the roots that slither through the walls. The inky pathways I have traced, they glow red and bright now, burn with a desperation, highlighting a route, showing me the way to her. Through the twisted concrete of this place, through every violent effigy, into the very centre of all this ruin, that is where I will find her, where I will find the beating black heart of this poisonous tree. It has her there, twisted in its tangle, coiled in its broken limbs. And I must kill it.

And yet hesitation. How can I trust this sound? What if all this is merely another trick? The fruit, the hospital, the map. I trusted it all, yet I was betrayed. I was laughed at.

Stay here and die then? Stay here and lie on the floor, thrash against the walls. For how long? An eternity of twisting. An eternity of never knowing. And that song, it makes me feel the way only she ever could. Nothing could imitate that.

And so into those dark, endless halls I go. Into those halls to find and destroy, not sit and wait. I feel my map in my veins. It burns my blood as I suck breath deep through the dust. It pumps harder and faster through me as I push further into the dark. I taste it in my throat. Sweat pink through my pores.

And I feel her song grow stronger with each step. I feel it in my flesh, in my gut. And the shudder of the tree, the reach of its branch, and wave after wave of nausea moves through me. I spew vile blackness into these dusty rooms and corridors. Leave a trail of thick shit, my chin dripping, mouth moving soundlessly, desperate shapes. I'm a tumbling mass of tangled limbs, rolling through the dirt here, falling against walls and fleeing. Falling against walls and searching.

All those words, my messages to her I left on these walls, they fade now. They blur away to grey and flake into the dark. Through the dust of rooms, the collapse of years, I struggle through brick and abandonment. I suck in the grit of old paint and plaster, coughing. I sleep in the corners of rooms, huddled against the cold as I leak, seep filth across the floor.

Those nights I rock to the pulse of her song, my body synchronising with her, locating the source so I may move on. I trace routes in the blackness that leaks from my body, plotting directions. Sometimes those shapes twist into new ones and I know I am being led astray.

In every room, along every hall, those spreading veins of tree grow thicker and throb blacker. I feel its thump shudder rhythmically through the building, through my body, a subsonic pulsing. It seeks me out, sucks on the dribbling sick I trail, drawing it down into its poisoned mass.

It is trying to stop me now, trying to fool me into false turns, blind corridors. Rooms change shape and location, hallways twist into new angles. I have to stop to allow the map to adjust, to allow her melody to find me and give me a fresh bearing.

I have been blind to so much for so long, the

sickness of its influence like a thick blanket. For a time it was comforting and safe, then it became suffocating. Now I want to be free of it, to shake it off and be with her again. And so I must vomit up that clotted lump of furry plaster that I have swallowed, that sits heavily in my gut.

Now in this place I am out of sight of windows, of daylight. I am beyond sky and fresh air. Deep within this tomb here, for days and days, trawling through the waste of my disease, the slip and slide of fat smeared on the walls, her song reverberates like a haunting tune from wall to wall. In this dark I chase her, but can never find her. In this dark I am chased by those roots. I can no longer avoid them. Every room I find to hide in is riddled through, marbled by veins of blue, the concrete cracking apart. I see gaps opening up everywhere. I smell the stench of rot emanating from those opening wounds.

I shout at the wall, cracking and cobwebbed with thin black. I rage and scream at the plaster, which flakes now and breaks, falls onto the bed. Blue thick sap now oozes from beneath the thin crumbling stone. I pick at that dry concrete, make a hole with my fist, punching, making bloody my hands on that wall.

The oozing increases with the widening hole,

plaster peels and flakes like dead old skin, and soon I am staring into the wall, into the ragged rent of stone and bile. And there is nothing there but the churning bruise of blue-black, a great sucking of air as it squirms, as it breathes. The horror of this place now, a vast concrete skin over a boiling black fat, a concentrated sickness that slithers and seethes through the dark. I feel it drawing air in, and expelling a foul breath, a rank stench that catches a metallic itch in my throat. And I gag, vomit on my knees over the dust of floor.

Now I can only watch as my own bloody blue bile is sucked down through the pores in the stone floor until nothing remains of it. I can see it being drawn down into the maelstrom of all this poison, down into the fat of my failure. I can see it melding, infusing, twisting into shapes. I can see hands and mouths emerging from the pitch. Out of that ruinous waste I can see figures of fat and bile.

Those hideous forms are clawing their way through the passages now, dragging feet slick with the inky vomit of guilt. They are sniffing their air, a pack of wild dogs. Those fists and feet scratch and claw, blackened skin glistens with their nightmare afterbirth.

And each face is mine. Each a copy in sick shapes.

They will find me in this place. They will find me and devour me, become me, multiply my form. They will make an army of me in fat. Those corrupt versions of me will spread their disease. They will infect all they encounter, and this vile black filth will never stop. The earth will be consumed by those roots, addicted to that sweet fruit. We will all succumb and fall. We will all fail.

So through the wall now, I go. I break through, into that sick twist of black and blue, a coiling sea of dark. Down through this mess, swimming, pulling through the viscous. My mouth fills with it, my throat, my lungs. I drown now in this shit, feel myself swelling with its cold, that sharp itch of iron courses along my veins. My body burns through this black.

Amongst this misery I will find the source of all this. I must pierce through this ocean of coagulation to reach that core, the solid centre that pumps this sickness through root and branch, that plants the seed in fruit and berry.

Hands and mouths reach and grab me. They bite and swallow. I feel tongues and lips curl around me, soft cold parts coil. I breathe this ink. Swallow and suck it down. It makes me sink deeper, taking me closer to the cause.

And I feel waves of it radiating out now, like gravity swells pulsing. Slowly at first, but increasing in frequency as I descend. My body shudders with each one, bones twist. The pressure makes my skull throb, but I push on, so close now.

And now I am surrounded by black. A great nothing. An intense emptiness pulling me in. Like an enormous lipless mouth, it sucks, and the hollowness I always felt inside me suddenly feels like a vacuum, and my body threatens to collapse into itself.

I would scream if I could. I would cry out and beg. But I am clogged. This fat of blue-black clings to my throat and lungs.

Then through that dark, through the swirling of noise and nothing, a coiling of limbs bleeds in. A churning of white, arms, legs, swimming in that terrible black, an emptiness now filling with something.

Hard edges emerge, twisting shapes, a dim light. Now a room, a damp apartment full of the twisting root of tree.

And that blackness gives way now to walls punctured through with the branches and roots, the invasion of that tree. Now to a floor, slick and wet with mold. Now to a bed, rotting with age.

She sleeps. Or appears to. Her skin is pale brown. Her lips black. Through her body the tree courses as a poison, an invading parasite. Her veins run with its brown blood. Her hair is brittle as bark. As I get closer, I smell the stench of damp leaves and autumn air.

And around her legs and arms the thick tendrils of tree wrap. They hold her close and tight. I know they can rip her apart. I know I have done this to her.

A milky light seeps into the room from one wall, a window by the bed covered with the slick brown tangles, a slithering mass of tentacles that squirm as if in pain to the soft white light.

I smash through all that mess. With bedside lamp, table, fists. I tear those roots away, blue-black sappy blood spraying.

From this ragged hole, I see it standing there in the small patch of yard, branches spread, witch fingers black and gnarled. From the window, I leap into its arms. I fall through, breaking against the great limbs, reaching out to snatch, to catch, to stop. My nails dig into the thick bark-skin, drawing gooey blue sap. I tumble to the hulk of trunk and slide down, embracing as I would my lover, though gnashing teeth in violent fury.

The earth opens up, a jagged maw, and swallows. Down into the roots and the dirt, the bleeding sap that fills my mouth now, with the black soil and oozing. I fight and thrash, my fists punching, nails clawing. I bite and I kick as the world falls in, as the sky turns blue and bleeds through black. Those slippery fibres, as deadly constricting snakes they coil, twist around me now, squeezing tight, my bones.

Up through now, up into the tangle of root and tuber. My mouth full of blue bleeding shit, punching my broken fists into the heart of that web. They break through into black plastic, and rotten blue-black mold spews out. It fills my mouth with rank filth, a cold like rusty metal. I try to spit and cough it out, but I swallow and feel it churn inside me as I dig and push, my body breaking through the ground, into the garden courtyard. I trail the oozing blood of tree sap like an afterbirth.

Shards of broken window glass lay strewn across the grass. My hands tighten around that cold sharp. My warm blood runs fresh now down my arms, hisses as it mixes with the sticky fluid of tree. I steam and fizz on the grass. Glow in the night.

Now my body radiates an aura in stuttering red and orange neon. I jump-cut in moments of violence. My killing urge is given focus, release.

I dig through bleeding. I rip into the body of my enemy. Blue-black pours out. How the world colours when viewed through the prism of ferocious action. How the world sounds, all hacking and stabbing and squelching. All else is silence and calm. Nothing but the frenzy. Nothing but the sound of desperate breath.

I feel it burning, my rage igniting in a brilliant hot. My wrath sears into meat of tree engulfs dry twists of bark and root, throwing me back to the grass with a wave of heat.

Now that burn tears through my veins, boils in my blood. Pin pricks of pain explode across my skin as my body writhes, white hot blood pushing through me, a cleansing fire I feel purging me of that addictive poison.

I spew up burning blue bile. It hisses and spreads out over the grass, steaming coils rising as spirit shapes. They flicker in the growing light of the tree aflame, the amber wall of tongue surging.

I choke and gag there on the ground, on my hands and knees. I feel a hard lump rising, something congealed being forced up out of me. My fingers claw into the soft earth as I struggle to bring it up. I feel it burning cold up my throat, and with a cry I vomit a clotted black lump of mold. It twists there on the grass in a slick slime of blue as I kick my legs to back away, wiping the traces from my lips. It sizzles in the heat, melts down, disintegrates. And I feel a space, a clean space, where it used to be inside me.

I watch it all burn. I watch the glowing sparks of orange rise into the air, a great cloud of drifting firebugs, popping and crackling into the night. Limbs of the tree burn through and collapse, falling to the earth with shuddering thuds and cracks that sound like bones breaking against stone. There is a yawning of ground, a cry of wood creaking and snapping as the hulk, now blackened and smouldering, falls, finally.

An eruption of ash and flame, the dying embers now in early dawn. There is a sound like a cry, the venting of hot air through the ground. This monster lies dead. It will churn with the dirt these days.

I return to her now, through the burning and groaning ground. I return to her in our apartment, the twisting black of root retreating, shrinking and smouldering, plaster dust filling the air with a fog.

I return to her on our bed. I curl with her amongst the covers, hold her cold body to mine. We lie there together, the sky outside ablaze, the apartment building now glowing orange as the raging fire spreads. It burns away the infection of tree, the branching and roots. A purging torrent of orange fury.

Through the halls, those blue marbled walls burst open with flame, concrete and plaster bubbles as old paint. Through the smoke and poison air, the heat that chases, doors buckle and twist. They pop with violent cracks and spit splinters.

She is free now of the roots, her colour returning, though still dreaming. Her song pulses still through the walls, the air; it throbs in my chest. Maybe we will become ash together, then we can be as one and forever drift on high winds. To be truly annihilated, to be seared to dust, a blackened relief against wall, blasted against concrete.

She opens her eyes and for a moment the fear that she will not know who I am is unbearable. Now she looks at me and I see the recognition. She moves her mouth to say my name and the sizzling hiss of burning timber fills the room.

We lie there, wrapped in limbs, coiled in cotton sheets. The fire rages around us. We watch everything blacken and reduce to ash. We feel no heat as the flames advance, as they grow closer and closer. We watch them and wonder.

We hold each other tightly. We await some destruction.

# About the Author

Kenny Mooney was born in Berlin when it was still divided by a stupid wall. He grew up in Scotland, England, and Cyprus. He is the author of the novels *Desk Clerk* and *In the Vast and Boundless Deep*. He lives in York.

www.kennymooney.com